Bantam Books in the Choose Your Own Adventure® Series
Ask your bookseller for the books you have missed

Choose Your Own Adventure Books for young readers

TREASURE DIVER

BY JULIUS GOODMAN

ILLUSTRATED BY PAUL GRANGER

An R.A. Montgomery Book

BANTAM BOOKS

TORONTO • NEW YORK • LONDON • SYDNEY • AUCKLAND

RL 6, IL age 10 and up

TREASURE DIVER
A Bantam Book / May 1984

Original conception of Edward Packard

ISBN 0-553-24050-1

Published simultaneously in the United States and Canada

PRINTED IN THE UNITED STATES OF AMERICA

O   0 9 8 7 6 5 4

**For those
who helped**

WARNING!!!

Do not read this book straight through from beginning to end! These pages contain many different adventures you can have as you dive for undersea treasure. From time to time as you read along, you will be asked to make decisions and choices. Your choice may lead to success or disaster!

Only you are responsible for your fate because only you can make these decisions. After you make each choice, follow the instructions to see what happens to you next.

Your adventures may lead to treasure or to your ruin. Think carefully before you make a move. Remember, the ocean is alive with danger.

Good luck!

SPECIAL WARNING AND VITAL DATA!!!

Scuba diving can be a safe and enjoyable sport, but it can also be a dangerous profession. In this book you are a certified scuba diver. Having undergone extensive training, you are familiar with the necessary underwater equipment. However, even the most experienced divers will always check their diving gear. In addition to your **wet suit, mask,** and **fins,** here is some of your equipment:

buoyancy compensator   Your buoyancy compensator pack is worn like a vest. It has a control that allows you to fill it with air from your tanks (or by mouth) to give you more flotation or to release air to reduce flotation.

instrument console   Attached to your tank by a flexible connector, the console has three gauges: a *compass,* a *depth gauge,* and a *pressure gauge.* The compass helps you navigate underwater. The depth gauge shows how deep you are. The pressure gauge measures the amount of air in your tanks; using your depth gauge and waterproof watch, you can figure out how much longer you can stay underwater. The back of your console is a slate. There is a pencil attached with which you can write messages to your diving buddy.

tanks and regulator   You wear a backpack containing two tanks of compressed air, enough for about an hour and a half of underwater time. Many factors determine precisely how long your air lasts. Your depth, how hard you are working or swimming, and even how cold the water is, are some of the factors that affect how much air you use. The regulator conducts air from your tanks to your mouth. It has three parts: the *mouthpiece* (which you hold with your teeth), the *hose*, and the *valve* on the tank. This valve also controls your reserve supply of air. When you have used up your main supply of air, you must push down a lever on the valve to release your reserve supply.

weight belt   Your weight belt has the proper amount of lead weights on it for you to counteract the buoyancy effect of water. A quick-release buckle enables you to remove it to help your ascent to the surface.

When diving for treasure you also have a **whistle** and **flares** for emergency use on the surface; a **knife** strapped to your leg; a **stainless steel probe rod** to pry things loose on the ocean bottom or to poke through the sand; and **mesh bags,** tied to your waist, for carrying things up to the surface or down to the bottom.

One of the greatest diving hazards you face has

many names—*decompression sickness, caisson disease,* or *the bends.* It is something you must always guard against. Under the great pressure of the water you are diving in, the nitrogen gas in the air you breathe is forced into your body. The deeper you dive and the longer you stay, the more nitrogen your body holds. If you surface with this gas in your body, the decreased pressure will cause bubbles to form (as opening a bottle of soda pop makes bubbles) and result in terrible damage. Decompression sickness may cause pain, blindness, paralysis, or death.

To avoid the bends, you must decompress slowly. Depending on how deep you dive and how long you stay, you will have to remain underwater at different shallow depths to allow the nitrogen gas to escape.

Nitrogen narcosis, or *rapture of the deep,* is another sickness that can result from the pressure on the nitrogen gas in your air. At depths of around 200 to 250 feet, extreme pressure turns nitrogen gas into a drug that causes symptoms of drunkenness. You may just feel happy—but you also may become confused and even pass out. Keep your wits about you!

"Will we ever find the treasure, Beech?" you say, leaning on the rail of the *Ocho Reales* and staring over the dark Gulf of Mexico waters reflecting the rising sun.

"Sure we will," Beech answers. Your friend and diving instructor is watching the hot Florida sunrise, too. "Just because for a week now we haven't found a trace of the sunken galleons doesn't mean that this next dive will be unsuccessful." He turns to you. "Why don't you get suited up? I'll get Macaulay and Kate."

Turn to page 2.

2

You can hear his footsteps as he walks across the deck, then below deck. Muffled shouts of, "C'mon, you guys, up and at 'em," drift up as you continue to gaze over the calm waters of St. John Bay. You remember the April afternoon two years ago when you were diving with Beech in the Florida Keys. Hidden in the coral you found the last rotting remains of a cloth sack. The sack contained black sea-corroded silver coins— Spanish pieces of eight. You used the four-hundred-year-old coins to buy the boat you own now, vowing to search for more treasure. You even named the boat *Ocho Reales,* taking the name from *reales de a ocho,* the Spanish term for "pieces of eight." Because of his expertise, Beech is captain, but as owner you make most of the decisions.

Beech has gone to get the rest of your crew. Macaulay is Bahamian, with years of both skin-diving and scuba-diving experience. Kate is also a diver and a good friend, but her most valuable asset is her capability in a library. She can find things that not even the librarian knows about. As your chief researcher, she helped you locate records of the Spanish fleet of 1698 that sank in a hurricane in this bay, littering the bottom with broken ships, dead men, and *tons* of gold and silver.

Turn to page 4.

At first you're not sure what it is. Then you realize that the shape isn't right. There is another boat alongside the *Ocho Reales*. You think it's probably just a fishing vessel, but its presence reminds you of Macaulay's warnings about pirates. "Where there is treasure," he'd said, "there are those who will stop at nothing to get it. I've seen some terrible things happen to people."

You also remember the warning of the Coast Guard lieutenant whose patrol boat visited yesterday: "A man known as Captain Jack has been seen in these waters. He's wanted on a number of charges and is extremely dangerous. I guess you could call him a pirate."

Could the boat alongside the *Ocho Reales* belong to pirates? The lieutenant said the pirates had been seen in a fifty-five-foot gray converted shrimper. That would be ten feet *longer* than the *Ocho Reales*. This boat is *shorter*; it can't be the pirates'—unless they've changed boats! Maybe you should go up and make sure.

On the other hand, you've barely started your dive, and that odd-shaped lump of coral is definitely worth investigating.

If you decide to surface to make sure everything is okay, go on to page 6.

If you decide to investigate the coral and let Beech handle the other boat, turn to page 10.

4

"Are you still standing there?" Beech's mock anger breaks into your reverie. "Don't just think about treasure, let's go get it!"

"Yeah! C'mon," Macaulay's cheery voice calls out. Laughing, you join your crew on the other side of the boat. After wriggling into your wet-suit jacket, you put on your flippers, weight belt, buoyancy compensator, and the rest of your equipment. Macaulay helps you put on your heavy tanks as Beech helps Kate. You and Kate will dive first this morning, while Beech and Macaulay remain on board in case you need help.

Go on to the next page.

All suited up, you and Kate lean backward off the small floating diving platform at the stern of the boat and fall back into the water. The scuba tanks on your back hit first with a splash, softening the impact on the rest of your body.

The weight of your equipment pulls you below the surface, and your mouth tightens on your hard rubber mouthpiece. You breathe naturally through it, forgetting about the sour taste. Kate comes into view, and you kick your flippered feet—slowly at first, then faster in your eagerness to reach bottom and find out if this spot holds treasure.

Turn to page 7.

Feeling regret at calling off the search before it has really started, you signal to Kate, pointing your thumb upward. "We're ascending," the divers' signal says. She looks surprised but signals back, "Okay."

You inflate your buoyancy compensator pack to help lift you to the surface and begin your ascent. As you approach the surface, you examine the boat alongside the *Ocho Reales*. From underwater it appears to be a perfectly ordinary sportfishing vessel, except perhaps for the larger than normal twin screws. Those propellers must be attached to huge engines; you know this would give the boat extraordinary speed.

You and Kate surface on the port side of your boat. Macaulay is waiting on deck. "Anything the matter?" he asks.

"What's that boat doing here? Didn't they see the 'divers down' flag?" You are referring, of course, to the large red square with the diagonal white strip flying high above the *Ocho Reales*'s deck. Any competent fisherman knows it means "Diver below; stay clear."

"I don't know," Macaulay answers, helping the two of you onto the deck. You stand there dripping sea water while he continues, "Captain Beech thinks they're ignorant."

"It looks like it," Kate snorts.

"Well, let's go take a look," you say, dropping your weight belt to the deck with a thud.

Turn to page 9.

The water darkens as the depth increases. You glance at your depth gauge: 50 feet. The fathometer on board the *Ocho Reales* showed bottom here at 90 feet. You kick a little harder, knowing that the sooner you reach the bottom, the more time you will have for exploration. But you know that you mustn't kick too hard, or you'll tire before your dive has even really started.

When the ocean bottom comes into view, you note the time on your waterproof watch. The bottom is quite smooth, with no deep crevices or caves in sight. Here and there are sea fans, and you spot other coral shapes as you kick around in a circle.

You carefully scan the bottom, knowing that years undersea can camouflage otherwise recognizable objects. You hope to find the coral-encrusted remains of a cannon or an anchor, clues to the presence of a sunken ship.

You kick in an ever-widening circle over the bottom. Nothing catches your eye at first; then you spot a lump of coral that looks odd in the hazy distance. Swimming over to investigate it, you look around to see if Kate has spotted the unusually straight lines of the coral, too. The bubbles rising from her regulator as she exhales draw your eyes upward. On the surface, 80 feet above, you can make out the outline of the *Ocho Reales*.

But something is wrong!

Turn to page 3.

"EXPLORE," you write on your slate and show it to Kate. She nods her head yes. Before you leave the cannon, you tie the long line of a marker buoy to it, activate the inflation mechanism, and watch the bright orange ball rise to the surface. You check the compass heading of the cannon, and after pointing out to Kate the direction you want to follow, you set off to explore the sea floor.

Kate swims at your left side. Your progress is slow because you each stop frequently, poking your probe rods into openings in the coral or into the sand bottom, hoping to hear the thump of wood or the ring of iron.

Turn to page 15.

You walk over to the starboard side of the *Ocho Reales,* where Beech is listening, not very patiently, to the captain of the fishing boat. A tall, thin man, his eyes are hidden beneath a white cap. "Listen," he says in a menacing tone, "get this floating trash heap out of here. These guys," he points a thumb at the two fishermen sitting in the fighting chairs on the afterdeck of his boat, "paid to fish here and they will, or my name ain't Bill Rounder."

Turn to page 12.

10

You swim over to Kate, pointing out the odd-shaped lump of coral. She can't really smile around her scuba mouthpiece, of course, but you can see the delight in her eyes as she signals, "Okay!"

You kick closer to the coral. Small schools of fish dart away as you come nearer. It's a cannon! You can hardly believe your luck—it's your first discovery in a week. The cannon is about seven feet long. It seems the right shape to have come from the 1698 fleet. The surface is thickly encrusted with coral, obscuring any date that might have been stamped into the metal. You will have to raise the cannon up to the *Ocho Reales* to clean it in order to learn more.

Turn to page 16.

Almost before the last word is out, Beech starts yelling back. You hate to get in the middle of this, but it seems like the only thing to do.

"Excuse me," you say, "maybe I can help."

"And who are you?" Captain Rounder thunders.

"I'm the owner," you answer.

"You?"

"Yes," you reply calmly. "I'd be happy to move if we could, but I'm not sure we can. Maybe we can help in another way." Beech stares at you, his eyes growing large. "Yesterday we were diving over in that area by the eastern shore, oh, about seventy degrees off the tip of the spit. A tremendous school of greater amberjack came in to feed. You might try fishing there."

Captain Rounder looks astonished; then he smiles. "Say, thanks. I'll give *you* some advice, too. About a half mile south of here along the reef, I've seen the remains of an old anchor. If you're diving for treasure," he gives a big wink, "you might try there." Then he becomes serious. "I'll give you another piece of advice. That bay is considered Captain Jack's territory. I wouldn't stay there any longer than I had to." He turns and, waving, motors off, heading toward the spot you recommended.

Go on to the next page.

"Whew!" Beech says. "That was good thinking. I'd forgotten about those amberjack." Then he realizes you've come up from diving. "What are you doing here?"

You laugh. "I saw another boat here and decided to come up and check it out. We didn't have a chance to see much down below. Some coral looked interesting, but it all does—until you take a close look."

Now Beech laughs. "Then I guess you'd better get below and take a close look at that coral. This may turn out to be the spot."

"Should we check out the spot Captain Rounder pointed out?" you wonder aloud.

"What about Captain Jack?" Macaulay asks. "I don't want to mess with him."

"That's all hooey," Beech answers. "He's a myth. There's no such person."

You're not completely convinced, but you're more concerned about where to dive.

If you decide to dive back down here, turn to page 17.

If you decide to move to the spot Captain Rounder suggested, turn to page 26.

You leave the bulk of the reef behind. Here and there you run into an outcropping of coral: huge, lacy gorgonians and other types of sea fans, or tremendous lumps of brain coral. Gradually the bottom becomes more and more sand.

You stop to check your pressure gauge and your watch. A quick calculation tells you that you have approximately forty-five minutes of air left. You look to see where Kate is. She's about ten yards ahead of you, still off to your left side, poking her rod into the sand. She turns, sees you, and raises her arms in a "now what" gesture, then swims ahead.

You hurry after her, not wanting to fall too far behind. Suddenly you are horrified to see Kate tumbling out of control and rolling rapidly to the right. She is caught in a powerful underwater current.

Turn to page 33.

16

You and Kate swim over the area around the cannon, poking your stainless steel probe rods into every lump of coral and hole in the ocean bottom. You find nothing more. Only the cannon is here to hint at treasure.

A glance at your watch shows you you've been down twenty minutes. You realize you can raise the cannon now and beat the time limit of thirty minutes at this depth for a no-decompression dive. You know that a dive where you have to decompress (to let out the nitrogen gas that water pressure has forced into your body) is always more dangerous than a no-decompression dive. Perhaps you should raise the cannon now. On the other hand, you are anxious to explore further.

If you stay down and explore,
turn to page 8.

If you attempt to raise the cannon,
turn to page 20.

You pick up your weight belt from the deck, buckle it around your waist, and announce, "We're diving here."

"Sounds good to me," Beech responds, and everybody else agrees.

Soon you and Kate are back in the water, heading for the bottom. You swim straight for the spot with the interesting coral. When you get close, you can see it *is* something from a sunken ship. It's a cannon! Your hunch to dive here again was right. Kate looks as excited as you are.

Turn to page 22.

18

You realize this is a dangerous position. The wake from this fast-moving boat will start the cannon rocking, and a ton of loose cannon can be lethal. It is also possible that the extra strain will snap the line, sending the cannon who knows which way and whipping the broken line around to do more damage

You don't know *why* this boat is headed toward you, but something tells you it's up to no good. You remember the Coast Guard lieutenant warning you that Captain Jack had a large gray converted shrimper and that he is extremely dangerous.

Turn to page 83.

"HEY, BEECH!" you yell as loudly as you can.

"That ought to get his attention," Kate says. She's right. Beech's head soon hangs out over the water.

"What are you doing here?" he asks.

"Just hanging around," you answer. "Nothing special. Do you have any sandwiches?" Beech's head quickly withdraws, then is replaced by Macaulay's friendly face.

"That sure was a short dive," he says, letting down a rope ladder. "Did you find it already?"

"Macaulay, what's going on?" Kate asks.

His grin fades. "This charter boat pulled up just after you left. Its skipper started yelling at us to get out of here. He said he always fishes here, and we had to move. Captain Beech told the other guy *he* had to move because we had divers below. He said, 'I don't see any No Parking signs.'" Macaulay laughs.

"Macaulay," you ask in a whisper, "are these guys pirates?"

Turn to page 25.

20

"RAISE CANNON," you write on your slate and show it to Kate. She signals, "Okay," with her hand. You reach into the bright yellow mesh bag clipped to your waist and pull out an inflatable buoy. After carefully tying the end of the line on the buoy to the cannon, you inflate the buoy and let it go. It shoots up to the surface, marking the cannon's location.

You raise your right thumb up in a signal to Kate. She nods and you rise slowly to the surface.

In a minute and a half you break the surface on the *Ocho Reales*'s port side. The other boat is still there; you saw the shape of its hull underwater as you ascended, but now your boat blocks it from your sight.

You spit out the regulator mouthpiece. You can clearly hear the loud words of an argument. "Listen," you say to Kate, who is floating by your side.

Turn to page 23.

You both swim around the cannon, breaking coral lumps off it with your probe rods. You decide to raise it to the surface where you can examine it more closely to make sure it's from the wreck you seek. On the boat, you can clean it to search for date marks. Here on the bottom, you can only tell that it is the right shape. From your experience you know the cannon weighs about two thousand pounds.

You and Kate surface and announce your find. There are shouts of joy from Beech and Macaulay. Kate goes back down with Beech, who is the expert at slinging up heavy objects to be lifted. Kate will make a sketch of the location of the cannon for later use in determining where to dive. You and Macaulay work the hoist. Below the water, Beech is attaching the hoist line to the cannon. Then come the two jerks on the line that you've been waiting for. You start the motor on the hoist and reel in the line, bringing the cannon to the point where it just floats.

"This should be easy," Macaulay shouts. "The sea is calm."

Slowly you raise the cannon until it's out of the water. The engine on the hoist strains as you haul the cannon up another foot. Macaulay moves over to the cannon to help guide it up.

You are about to engage the hoist again to raise the cannon and swing it over onto the *Ocho Reales*'s deck when something off to the side catches your eye. A large gray boat is headed your way at high speed.

Turn to page 18.

"Look, I don't know how many times I have to tell you," Beech's angry voice is saying, "that flag up there," your eyes are involuntarily drawn to the large red square with the diagonal white stripe flying high over the *Ocho Reales,* "means we have divers below. It's dangerous for you to be here. Now shove off!"

You can't hear any reply from the other boat. You try yelling, but there's no answer. You want to get on your boat, but there's no boarding ladder on the port side, and you can't pull yourself onto the deck in your heavy equipment. You could climb onto the diving platform at the stern, but you're a little worried about just swimming over there unannounced. The other boat may have lines in the water that you could get tangled in, or if it took off quickly, the wash from the propellers could be dangerous. You're anxious to get on the boat. You want to find out what's happening, and you're eager to start raising the cannon.

If you try yelling again to get attention, turn to page 19.

If you decide that yelling's no good and you must swim to the platform, turn to page 40.

"Deeper for Kate. Deeper for Kate," you think, as you kick downward. The water becomes even darker; you can hardly see. Your legs continue to kick, but they feel rubbery and not really a part of you.

You giggle; then you laugh. "Of course I can't find Kate; it's too dark," you think. "I'd better call to her." "Kate!" you shout, until you realize she can't hear you with the silly rubber thing in your mouth. You pull it out and call again. "Kate!"

The bubbles of your last breath of air rise to the surface 280 feet above. There is no answer to your shout, but you don't care.

The End

"I thought so at first, but I don't think so now," he answers. "There are just three of them. The captain and the two fishermen he's taking out."

You drop your weight belt onto the deck and, shrugging out of your tanks, head over to where Beech is again yelling at the other boat captain.

"Morning," you call across to the skipper of the other boat when you can get a word in. A tall, thin man, he glares at you from under his white hat, then barks, "And who are you?"

"I'm the owner," you reply.

"Well then, get this boat out of here," he snaps. He goes on to tell you that he always brings fishermen to this spot; he catches a lot of fish there. The *Ocho Reales* is in his way and must move.

You look closely at this man and look over his boat and passengers. These people can't be the pirates you were warned about. They look barely capable of baiting a hook. You consider the captain's request, although you know you really don't have to move. You think that if you're too stubborn about moving, these men might start to wonder why you're there and spread rumors. Better to keep your treasure diving a secret.

"We'll move," you say.

Turn to page 44.

"Let's get underway," you announce. "I want to dive on the reef where Captain Rounder spotted that old anchor."

"What about here?" Kate asks.

"We can come back to it," you answer. "It's not going anywhere." You all pitch in, hauling up the anchor and securing the diving platform, and soon you are anchored in the spot pointed out by Captain Rounder, ready to dive again.

"C'mon, Kate," you say, "let's go find the treasure." Beech and Macaulay watch as you sink below the surface again. Dropping swiftly through the water, you stop at the base of the reef, 100 feet down here. Your eyes are drawn up the slope of limestone reef. Somehow, you are sure this is where you will find the remains of the wrecked fleet and its precious cargo of gold and silver.

SILVER

PIECES OF EIGHT

Turn to page 31.

"Okay, Beech," you say. "No air lift, at least for a while."

"All right!" he whoops. "Let's go, Macaulay." They rush into their diving gear and head into the water. You and Kate clean up your gear, rinsing it with fresh water and hanging it to dry. Above all, though, you keep an eye on the water, watching the twin sets of air bubbles from Beech and Macaulay for any sign of trouble.

When they finally come back on board, they look disappointed.

"Nothing," Macaulay says.

That night, having tired yourselves out, you all sleep well. At seven the next morning you assemble for the day's diving.

You and Kate are first in the water again. It feels cold this early, but you soon get used to it. The next logical spot to explore is just north of the spot you examined yesterday. The current runs north, and the treasure must have drifted with it. You and Kate start at the bottom of the reef wall again, rising slowly to the top. Again you poke your stainless steel probe rods everywhere, looking for any hint of the treasure ships. You find nothing of interest except for the same grouper that watched you yesterday.

Turn to page 47.

"Let's get out of here," you motion to Kate. You swim into the small tunnel. It seems longer and darker than before, and you worry that you and Kate may have been detected by the inhabitants of the hide-out. Finally, though, you kick out into the blue sea and back to the *Ocho Reales.* You are anxious during your decompression. The water doesn't seem as friendly to you as it normally does; there is menace in it.

When your decompression is done, you ascend, but in your eagerness to get on board your boat, you rise right into the tentacles of a Portuguese man-of-war jellyfish.

The long thin tentacles brush against your bare arms and face. The stinging cells release their burning poison. Knowing better, but disoriented with the pain, you rub against the poisonous stingers in an attempt to remove them. That releases more poison, causing more pain.

Finally you swim clear of the entangling tentacles and, in agony, rise to the surface. Beech and Macaulay are there wearing rubber gloves, having been alerted by Kate—who watched helplessly, afraid of getting stung herself.

You scream with pain until the sedative Beech gives you takes affect. He and Macaulay wash the stung parts of your body with alcohol while Kate heads the *Ocho Reales* toward shore—and the nearest hospital—as fast as possible. You won't be diving again for a long time.

The End

You examine the base of the reef carefully. There is no sign of any galleon anchor. You and Kate slowly swim up the reef, poking here and there with your probe rods and disturbing crabs, lobsters, triggerfish, and others that live in holes and small caves in the coral. Today, the incredibly colorful and prolific display of reef life fails to dazzle you. Today, you are looking for straight lines, spheres, and even the gleam of gold.

You hear a sharp tapping while you carefully skirt the opening in the reef that a mean-looking moray eel has claimed as home. You look up. Kate is tapping her tank with her stainless steel probe rod to get your attention. Careful not to disturb the razor-toothed moray, you swim over to where Kate points at a round object surrounded by the short stumps of finger coral. She pokes at it with her rod. It's a cannonball! You are on the right track.

Excitedly you and Kate explore the area around the cannon ball. You feel a bump on the shoulder and look up to see a huge grouper hanging over you. Lazily fanning its fins, it stares at you, a look of intense curiosity in its eyes. You turn back to the crevice you have been exploring. Something glints in there! You reach your hand in and pull out a gold necklace, perfectly intact.

Turn to page 58.

"Okay, Beech," you say. "We'll all dive."

As you hit the water, your nervousness about leaving the *Ocho Reales* is replaced by eagerness to explore. The four of you fan out in a search pattern. After ten minutes, you finally come across the cannon again. It blends in so well with the coral on the bottom that you can't believe you found it so easily the first time. You bang on your air tanks with your stainless steel probe rod to attract the others.

Beech gives the cannon a once-over, then grins around his mouthpiece and flashes the "okay" sign. He and Macaulay get to work with a line, tying the cannon in a sling so it can be lifted out of the water. Kate floats nearby, sketching the ocean bottom on a waterproof slate to show the terrain and the exact placement of the cannon. The drawing may be useful for later exploration.

Meanwhile, you swim over the bottom in the nearby area, looking for other clues to the treasure. You swim in a circle around the canon, widening the diameter each time around to look at new territory. About twenty feet away from your friends, on your last pass, you notice sharks.

Turn to page 43.

You kick your feet, the flippers driving you powerfully forward. You've got to keep Kate in sight. You can just maintain pace with the current; Kate is about fifty feet ahead of you now, still tumbling. She still has her mouthpiece in place; at least she can breathe. Your legs and arms are tiring fast.

You realize suddenly that the exertion of chasing her will use up your air supply more rapidly. You're at 120 feet and the bottom slopes downward from here. Also, the farther you swim away from the boat, the more air you will need to get back. And the deeper you go, the faster you will use up your air. You could slip into the current that caught Kate and travel with it. Perhaps you can keep control and catch up to her. Or should you head back to the boat and get fresh air-tanks and help?

If you try to slip into the current that caught Kate, turn to page 53.

If you head back to the boat, turn to page 36.

"I'm going in," you signal to Kate. She shakes her head no. You write on your slate, "WAIT HERE 5 MIN—" but before you can finish, Kate grabs the slate out of your hands and writes, "GOING WITH YOU." Quickly—before either of you loses courage—you swim up to the entrance. Climbing up the steel ladder dropping out of the hole, you pull yourself up three feet into the building and air.

After spitting out your regulator and pushing your mask up to your forehead, you climb the rest of the way, stepping onto a steel deck around the opening.

Scuba equipment lines one curved side of a medium-sized room; four tanks and regulators hang on the hooks. On the opposite wall is a closed, watertight bulkhead door.

"What's that?" Kate whispers, pointing to a pile of small plastic bags on one side of the room.

Go on to the next page.

You walk quietly over and pick one up. You pull apart the plastic, and some rough pebbles tumble into your hand. Here and there they glint strangely green. You see a small label on the bag: "Bogotá, Colombia." From what you've heard and read, you realize with a shock that these must be emeralds. "Smuggled gems!" you whisper back.

"Let's get out of here!" Kate responds. That's your thought, too; you've seen enough. You turn to go, and your eyes fall on the closed bulkhead door. What's behind that?

If you decide you can't resist opening the door, turn to page 99.

If you decide you'd better leave now, turn to page 51.

Knowing the dangers you risk, you head to the surface. You kick rapidly, steering up, away from Kate, who continues down into the depths. You turn the control valve on your buoyancy compensator. Air from your tanks rushes into the vest and helps speed you to the surface. You know you're going up too fast, but you must get help.

You shoot out of the water, your head and chest popping into the air. You spot the *Ocho Reales* about one hundred feet away, but you're in agony. Your lungs feel as if they'll burst from the excess air. Your joints are on fire. You know that if nitrogen bubbles form in your brain or spinal cord, paralysis, blindness, or convulsions will result.

You spit out your mouthpiece, but your voice won't work. You can't yell! You remember the emergency signal flares in the pocket of your pack, but the pain is too great for you to move enough to reach them. You can't even reach the whistle tied within easy reach to your regulator hose. You are bent almost double with pain, but your brain still works—so far.

If you choose to stay on the surface, hoping you'll be spotted from the boat, turn to page 60.

If you try to repressurize by diving, turn to page 73.

"Macaulay, we're going through the islands."

"Okay," Macaulay says, shaking his head. The coral islands are really part of a large reef off the tip of the spit. About a mile square, the reef pokes up out of the water here and there. There are channels through the coral, but they're not marked, and the water in most of the maze is too shallow for a big boat to get through. Sometimes, though, it can be done. You hope this is one of those times; if you don't make it, you'll run into a coral head, a hard, sharp, growth of coral that will rip a hole in the *Ocho Reales* and sink it. Then you'll be at the mercy of Captain Jack.

"There they are!" Macaulay shouts as the islands come into view.

"Quick, run up forward and tell me where to turn," you shout back. You glance over your shoulder at the two pursuit boats. They're gaining on you.

"Slow down! Slow down!" Macaulay shouts. You throttle back, then follow Macaulay's shouts of "Left! Left again! Hard right!" You enter the heart of the reef.

Turn to page 39.

You can only go so fast and still have time to turn as Macaulay directs. You wonder if it's fast enough. You look behind you again. The smaller, white boat follows you into the reef. The gray boat heads around to meet you on the other side when you come out. Then Macaulay shouts, "Back! Back! Back!"

You throw the boat into reverse. The engines roar. The *Ocho Reales* slowly, slowly loses speed, then runs aground. You're trapped!

Turn to page 110.

"Stay here," you say to Kate, who is now hanging on to the side of the *Ocho Reales*. "I'll swim over and see what's going on."

Using the breast stroke, you swim away. As you reach out to grab a corner of the diving platform, you hear the engines of the other boat. There is a strong stink of diesel fuel; then you are violently shoved by the wake of the departing fishing boat. Your hand grabs nothing but air as you clutch for the platform, and your head slips under, giving you a noseful of water. You try not to panic and kick upward, thinking that in a moment the surface will be calm enough for you to try for the platform again.

Suddenly you're moving rapidly through the water, tangled in a line from the fishing boat. You twist like a top as the boat drags you face forward through the water at twenty knots. You cannot reach your scuba mouthpiece, and you rapidly drown.

The End

Your heart leaps in panic, but you force yourself to act calmly. You know that sharks are terribly overrated as a diving menace. It is extremely rare that a diver is attacked by a shark. Still, it's wise to take precautions. As you swim back to your friends, you wonder what attracted these sharks to this spot. You look back at them. There are more now. You can see vertical stripes on their sides. The largest is about thirteen feet long and has very faint stripes, a sign of its age. You recognize the species—tiger sharks. They move so quickly it is hard to count them, but it looks as if there are at least eight.

As you approach Macaulay, Kate, and Beech, you see what has attracted the sharks. Great pieces of bloody fish are floating down from the surface. You look up in horror. A fishing boat floats overhead, dropping chum. A time-honored trick of fishing, chumming is used to attract fish, which can then be caught on baited hooks. You wonder frantically if this is the same fishing vessel the *Ocho Reales* tangled with this morning. Did *they* take your marker? Do they know you're here?

Turn to page 45.

Beech starts to argue, but you stop him with a hand on his arm. You turn back to the fishermen. "We can move for you now, but I can't guarantee we can do it again. We are starting some scientific exploration here. When we're in the middle of it, we can't be disturbed." You figure that's only a little white lie.

"Well, all right," the fishing boat captain replies. "We'll work out something else later." You wonder if that "something else" involves you, but you don't say anything. The boat motors slowly away.

As you and the rest of the crew get ready to leave you explain to an angry Beech why you didn't want the fishing boat to be too curious. He understands, but he hates losing an argument.

Turn to page 70.

The rest of your diving group watches the sharks as you join them. You know that the sharks will go on a feeding frenzy in minutes, and that you'd better be out of there. You have heard of sharks so crazed by blood in the water that they'll continue to feed even while another shark eats them.

You motion to the others to follow you away when one of the sharks darts toward a chunk of fish. Suddenly they're all around you. The water turns red with blood as the sharks tear at anything they can get their teeth into—including the four of you.

The End

A glance at your watch and pressure gauge, and a quick calculation, tell you that there isn't enough time to head back up the reef at another spot, so you write a note to Kate: "EXPLORE BASE OF REEF," pointing in the direction you want to go. She acknowledges and heads off. You tag after, staying farther away from the reef than she does, so as not to cover the same ground.

You search for some time before something catches your eye near some big rocks—a glint of gold. You swim over to investigate, but it turns out to be nothing but coral—and your imagination. You try to swim away and realize you can't. You're stuck!

You start to panic, but your training takes over. You reach up to see what's holding you. Fishing line! It's snagged all over the rocks and now you're caught in it. No problem, you realize. You can cut yourself free with your knife.

You reach down to your leg and unsheathe your knife. Then everything seems to happen at once. A shark swims by, and, startled, you drop your knife. Then you run out of air!

Turn to page 86.

"Oh, no," you say. "I bet they're connected with Captain Jack."

Macaulay peers at the white boat through the binoculars, then says, "They've got guns and they look mean."

"We'd better figure out how to get out of here," you answer. You turn the radio on; you've been too busy up till now to use it. "Calling the Coast Guard, this is *Ocho Reales,* N89FPY. This is an emergency."

"This is the Coast Guard. We read you loud and clear, *Ocho Reales.*"

"We are being pursued by two boats. A fifty-five-foot gray converted shrimper and a white thirty-five-foot sport fisherman. Can you lend assistance?"

There is a short whistle from the guardsman you're speaking to. Then, "Captain Jack, huh? We've been after him for a long time. What's your position, *Ocho Reales?*"

"We're headed north, out of St. John Bay, maybe three minutes from the coral islands. They're gaining on us. How soon can you get here?"

Go on to the next page.

"We're on our way now. About thirty minutes."

"Probably too late, but we'll try to hold on. *Ocho Reales* out." You turn to Macaulay, who looks as scared as you feel. "The coral islands are right off the tip of this spit," you say. "If we head for them, those boats might not want to follow us through."

"But we could run into a coral head," Macaulay responds. "We'd rip out the bottom of the boat."

"I think it's worth a try—I think it's our only chance."

"I saw something on TV once," Macaulay says slowly. "It was the same kind of situation. Two chase boats were closing in from opposite directions on this other boat."

"What happened?"

"The other boat kept in the middle until the last possible second, then pulled away. The two chase boats rammed each other." Macaulay's eyes glow at the thought.

If you try to lure the two boats into each other, turn to page 78.

If you try to get through the coral maze, turn to page 37.

50

It's Beech! You start to signal that you're out of air, but he knows it. He hands you a fresh tank. Greedily you suck at it. The oxygen feels wonderful. Then you spot Macaulay with Kate.

You swim to the boat, gradually ascending, traveling the last five minutes at 40 feet. You carefully watch your body for any signs of the bends, but you feel nothing. Your joints don't ache, your limbs don't feel shaky or numb; you feel okay.

At the boat you all rise to 30 feet. Macaulay continues to hold Kate while Beech goes up to ready the recompression chamber. You are thankful now that you spent the money to get one. It will hold only one person; you will have to stay underwater for the prescribed length of time in order to avoid the bends.

Kate is taken aboard and put into the chamber. The transfer is made swiftly, and Beech is immediately on the radiotelephone to a doctor about her condition.

Turn to page 54.

"Hurry!" you say to Kate. "We're leaving." She climbs down the ladder first. As you turn to follow her, you spy a small metal chest near the entrance. You grab it, thinking it might contain some evidence to prove that all this is real. Just before submerging, you glance around the room again. The locking wheel on the watertight door—it's turning!

You and Kate swim away from the habitat at top speed. When you reach the tunnel you look back. You see no one following you, but somehow you feel pursued.

Turn to page 56.

You kick hard to the right and slip into the current that caught Kate. The turbulence is powerful. You feel as if you're being hit all over with rubber hammers, but by keeping your arms extended in front of you and by kicking steadily, you are able to maintain control.

You're gaining on Kate. She is now only ten yards away. It looks as if she keeps trying to stop herself. You want to shout: "No! Straighten out! Go with the flow, *then* kick out." But you can't. There's no way you can get the message to her.

The bottom has leveled out. A glance at your depth gauge shows you're at 150 feet. You look back up and spot it: a huge, gaping black hole in the sea floor—and the current is carrying Kate right into it! She disappears from sight.

You try to pull out of the current, away from the dark hole that swallowed Kate, but it's impossible. The current is like a cage, and you, too, are swept down into the dark.

Turn to page 64.

It feels good to you when you can move up to the 20-foot level. Some more time here, then some more at 10 feet, then back on board. It almost feels like you've made it already. In addition to fresh bottles of air, Macaulay keeps sending down notes on a slate tied to a line. Some of them are short jokes. Most are designed to be morale boosters while you wait and worry about your diving buddy. But the best morale booster of all is the one that reads: "KATE'S OK."

The End

"Beech, I think one of us should remain on board," you say. "Don't forget them." You point to the fishing boat, which is now moving slowly to the south of you.

"Them?" Beech asks. "They're no problem, but maybe you have a point. Since you're the one with the bright idea, I guess it's you who stays. I'm sure everybody else would rather dive."

"I'll stay, too," says Kate.

Beech looks surprised, then shrugs his shoulders. "We'll only stay down thirty minutes. I don't want to bother with decompression. Come on, Macaulay." They soon splash into the water. You watch the twin set of bubbles from their exhalations come up. As Beech and Macaulay dive deeper, the interval between each group of bubbles gets longer. You can tell when they are on the bottom because the bubbles rise at regular intervals.

Turn to page 61.

56

Back in the open ocean, your heart pounding, you hurry back to the *Ocho Reales*. When you arrive, there are fresh air-tanks and a slate hanging into the water from the boat. You and Kate change your almost exhausted tanks for the fresh ones. On the slate is a note from Beech asking for a diagram of your time underwater. It's a standard diving technique, something you've done many times, but as you draw the diagram that will show the length of time you've spent at different depths, your hand shakes. Beech will use the complete decompression tables on the boat to determine how long you must stay underwater to avoid the bends.

WHAT'S YOUR DIVE PROFILE?

Go on to the next page.

You send the slate up and wait for what seems like a long, long time. Kate seems as nervous as you, but you know that, in a weird way, that's good. Fear causes an increase in heartbeat and breathing rates, helping to get rid of the nitrogen gas more quickly.

Finally, the slate comes down. "YOU'VE BEEN AT 20 FT LONG ENOUGH. COME UP TO 10 FT FOR 40 MIN."

You and Kate exchange glances. Then you grab the slate and write: "TOO LONG! WE'VE GOT TO GET OUT OF HERE! EMERGENCY!!! WE MUST LEAVE HERE AS QUICKLY AS POSSIBLE. RECALCULATE FOR MINIMUM DECOMP TIME." The slate is drawn up as you move to the 10-foot level.

The slate finally comes back down. It reads: "ABSOLUTE MINIMUM IS 23 MIN BUT BENDS IS DANGER. STILL SUGGEST 40 MIN."

You look at your watch. "Well, that's it," you think. You've been at 10 feet for three minutes. Twenty minutes to go. And when you surface you risk the bends. But if you stay down long enough to avoid risking the bends, you risk a visit from Captain Jack—or whoever was opening that door.

If you decide to stay down for twenty more minutes, turn to page 71.

If you decide to stay down for the full forty minutes, turn to page 69.

Even in the dull underwater light, the necklace looks remarkable. About two feet long, it is composed of many tiny links. You put it inside your wet suit for safekeeping. Then you and Kate spend nearly an hour examining a wide area around the crevice where you found the necklace, but you find nothing more.

You continue upward, looking with renewed vigor. Swimming around a large bulge in the coral wall, you discover a wide opening. A coral cave! You peer in, but see nothing except for a faint bluish light at a distance. You wonder if an opening in the coral farther up lets light into the cave. Could there be treasure in the cave?

Go on to the next page.

You check your pressure gauge and depth gauges. You're at 40 feet. You have enough air left to explore the cave a bit but, depending on what's in it, probably not completely. Maybe you should go back to the *Ocho Reales* now; you'd love to see Beech and Macaulay's faces when you show them the necklace. Later, you can come back to the cave with full tanks. On the other hand, you're here now, and the mystery of what may be in the cave beckons.

If you decide to explore the cave,
turn to page 74.

If you decide to come back to the cave later,
go on to page 62.

You pray the *Ocho Reales* is on the lookout for you and Kate. You double up again from cramps. "C'mon, Beech, Macaulay," you think, "you've got to spot me."

A nitrogen bubble forms in one of your carotid arteries, cutting off blood circulation to half of your brain. You go into convulsions and die.

Beech and Macaulay find your floating body ten minutes later. Kate too is lost. They have no idea where she is, and their searching is fruitless.

The End

"Well, they're down," you say to Kate. "I guess we'd better get our equipment together." Keeping one eye on the water and another on your watch, you prepare the equipment for your next dive. You exchange your empty air-tanks for full ones, and check over each tiny piece for any problems.

When you're finished you look at your watch: twenty-one minutes. Beech and Macaulay will be down for nine more minutes. "I wonder if they've found anything," Kate says.

"We'll know soon," you reply, pointing to your watch.

"Sooner than you thought," Kate says, spotting a rush of bubbles breaking on the surface. "They must have found the cannon! Beech wouldn't come up early unless they were successful."

Beech's head pops out of the water. He spits out his mouthpiece, shouting, "Macaulay's in trouble! We found the cannon. His foot's caught under it, and I can't get it free. Throw me a line. I'll tie it around the cannon, then signal you to winch it up."

It sounds like a good idea, but you might be able to free Macaulay more quickly if you went down to lend a hand instead.

If you throw Beech the line, turn to page 68.

If you tell Beech you'll go down with him instead, turn to page 91.

You swim over to Kate and point your thumb upward in the divers' signal for "We're ascending." Reluctantly she follows you back to the *Ocho Reales*. Suspended in the water waiting for you are fresh tanks of air and a slate for messages. You exchange your nearly empty tanks for full ones and send a note up to Beech describing your dive depths and the length of time you spent at those depths. He sends the slate back down with a note that you must wait at 20 feet for two minutes, then at 10 feet for forty-one minutes. You settle back to wait, wishing you had a waterproof copy of a good book.

"Find anything?" Macaulay eagerly asks when you're finally back on board.

"Just this," you say, slowly pulling the necklace out from its safekeeping spot under your wet-suit top. The two-foot-long chain glints dully in the sunlight. You discover that each fine link is engraved with a leafed vine. You realize with a start that the necklace is back in the open air for the first time in almost three hundred years. You wonder who wore it, what they thought of the necklace, and what kind of life they lived. Beech turns it over and over in his hands, repeating, "I can't believe it." Macaulay, too, is a little stunned—as are you and Kate. After a week of searching, you've finally found treasure here. You shout it out loud, "Treasure!"

Go on to the next page.

Eventually you all calm down. Beech and Macaulay are ready to explore the spot on the reef where you found the necklace and cannonball. But you're not so sure. "Beech," you say, "I had a lot of time to think while we were decompressing. We might find some more treasure on the reef where we found the necklace. But I think the ship itself is really under the sand bottom below the necklace site. The ship probably hit the reef and sank, tumbling treasure down the face of the reef and coming to rest at the bottom. We need to explore the face of the reef and the sand bottom at its base. That's where we'll find the heavy treasure—the silver and gold."

"Whew," Kate says, "I didn't do any of that heavy thinking."

You laugh, then Beech asks, "I suppose you're talking about using the air lift."

Turn to page 66.

The speed of the current increases. You don't need to look at the depth gauge to know you are being drawn deeper and deeper: your ears ache and your mask is being squeezed tighter against your face. It's dark, and that adds to the terror.

Inexplicably the current eases, and you are able to swim to one side, out of it. You float in one spot, deep in the hole, trying to slow down your breathing. Above you can see the bright opening. Where is Kate?

You look down at the glowing dial of your depth gauge: 200 feet! You can't stay at this depth for long.

Go on to the next page.

A little light filters down through the hole above. You don't think you passed Kate on the way down, so she must be below you. You reach into a pocket and pull out an underwater flashlight. If you shine it down, Kate will see it and swim to it. Then you realize that she might be injured and unable to swim to the light. Kate might even be unconscious or suffering from nitrogen narcosis—"rapture of the deep." She might be so intoxicated by the effects of the pressure that even if she sees the light she may not know what to do about it. Maybe you should venture deeper to look for her, though it means risking more exposure to "raptures" and decompression problems yourself. It's so hard to think! Maybe *you* are beginning to feel the effects of the pressure.

If you go deeper to look for Kate, turn to page 88.

If you try the flashlight, hoping Kate will swim toward it, turn to page 102.

66

"'Fraid so, Beech." As you say it, though, you're beginning to have second thoughts. The air lift is a simple mechanism. A long, six-inch-diameter hose runs from the ocean bottom up to the surface. Another, smaller, hose runs with it, carrying compressed air from the compressor on the deck of the *Ocho Reales*. The compressed air is fed into an opening at the bottom of the large hose. This creates suction at the mouth of the large hose. If you hold the end of the large hose near the ocean bottom, it sucks up water, sand, fish, small rocks, gold, silver, and anything else it runs into. What it picks up is carried up to a sorting tray floating on the surface and is sifted for valuables. The air lift's virtue is that you can explore a large area for treasure in a small amount of time.

Its vices are numerous. It is hard to control; if you lose track of the mouth for a second, it buries itself in the sand. Then you have to turn off the air lift, dig it out, clean it out, and start again. It also has a tendency to try to eat too much and clog up; then it has to be turned off, cleaned out, and started over again.

Go on to the next page.

The air lift is also dangerous. It's so powerful that if an arm is sucked squarely over the opening, the air lift will pull the blood right through the skin. On top of all that, the compressor on the boat makes an awful racket. But it does let you sift through an incredible amount of bottom looking for treasure.

"Can't I talk you out of using it?" Beech asks. "At least for a while? We still have a lot of bottom to explore. Who knows what we'll find. Maybe we won't have to use that noisy, dangerous thing after all."

If you decide to forget about using the air lift—at least for now—turn to page 27.

If you still want to use the air lift, turn to page 84.

68

You throw the winch line to Beech. He takes one end down while you watch the line wind off the drum on the large hoist at the *Ocho Reales*'s stern.

Minutes pass before you see two tugs on the line, Beech's signal to take up the slack. Slowly you wind the line in, stopping when you feel resistance. Beech surfaces several minutes later. "It's all set," he shouts. "Take it up slowly about three feet." While you haul in the line, Beech dives again.

When you've reeled in three feet of line, you stop, waiting for more instructions. Kate stands ready to help, staring intently at the water. "Beech is coming back up!" she shouts. You're ready to do whatever he asks. Then Kate shouts, "It's Macaulay!" You feel weak with relief.

As you help Macaulay on board, Beech swims over. "I've got to go mark the spot where the cannon was." You check your watch: thirty minutes—the whole incident didn't take long. But, in some odd way, you feel as if it did. "You might want this," Beech interrupts your thoughts, handing you what looks like a chunk of black rock. "It was under the cannon." Then he dives and is gone.

Turn to page 106.

"We can't risk the bends," you think. You write on the slate: "40 MIN. HAVE BOAT READY TO LEAVE AS SOON AS WE SURFACE" and show it to Kate. She nods, then you send the slate up to Beech.

When twenty minutes have passed, you begin to have second thoughts. You wish the bends weren't such a risk. With each passing minute, you find it harder to stick to your decision and stay down for the full decompression time.

Finally you can't stand to wait any longer. You turn to signal to Kate that you're ascending early—and spot four divers heading toward you on scooters.

You try to escape, but you can't outrace their spear guns. The sharp-tipped spears heading straight for you are the last thing you'll ever see.

The End

Hours later you get back to your site. Macaulay is the first to discover that the buoy marking the cannon is no longer there.

"He must have cut the line," Beech yells, his face darkening. "Why, I'll get that . . ."

"It's no big deal," you interrupt Beech. "Kate and I found the cannon easily, before, and we can do it again."

"Well, we'll all go down," Beech responds, cooling off a little. "We've lost too much time already today. The four of us can do more work."

It sounds like a reasonable idea, but you're still nervous about that fishing boat, which is slowly motoring south of you, deeper into the small bay you're in. They may not be pirates, but you still don't like the looks of them. If you all dive, no one will be left on board the *Ocho Reales*. That might not be a good idea.

If you agree with Beech's plan to have everyone dive, turn to page 32.

If you feel you must leave someone on board the Ocho Reales, *turn to page 55.*

Even twenty minutes may be too long. You look at the metal chest hanging in the bright yellow mesh bag clipped to your waist. Maybe you shouldn't have taken it.

You take the big slate and write another message to Beech. "WE STAY 20 MIN. READY RECOMPRESSION CHAMBER—AND BOAT FOR QUICK GETAWAY." You don't let Kate see the message before you send it up to Beech. You take your slate and write a note to Kate: "WE STAY 40 MIN." You hate lying to her. Her eyes grow large as she nods. You know that this way she'll stay scared and rid herself of the nitrogen gas faster.

You look at your watch every few minutes. Time passes so slowly. You keep looking around, but nobody comes swimming after you. You listen carefully, but hear only the sound of the bubbles from the regulators and the occasional thump of something happening on the *Ocho Reales.*

Turn to page 94.

"Macaulay!" you shout. "Quick! Cut the cannon free, then drop some scuba tanks for Kate and Beech." You hear the snap of the wire rope as the hoist drops its one-ton burden. You glance at the position of Captain Jack's boat, then pull the *Ocho Reales*'s throttle to the maximum. There is a tremendous roar; then your boat leaps forward. You look back to see the cannon slowly sinking and the gray boat gaining on you.

"Let's go!" Macaulay shouts, as he runs forward after dropping the scuba tanks overboard. But you're going as hard as you can. You look back to see Captain Jack's boat swerving.

"They're avoiding the cannon," Macaulay yells.

"Good! It gives us the time we need," you shout back. Your boat shoots ahead, finally gathering enough speed to start planing. The *Ocho Reales* is almost flying over the water now, swiftly leaving Captain Jack's boat behind.

"What do we do now?" Macaulay says, coming up to your side.

"I don't know," you answer. "Got any good ideas?"

"No, but I've got bad news." Macaulay points. You are almost out of the small bay. Bearing down on you from the north is a white boat.

Turn to page 48.

In agony, you take a deep breath and pull the emergency dump valve on your buoyancy compensator. The air rushes out as you sink beneath the water. Ten feet, then twenty feet, and the pain eases. You are able to find your regulator, insert it into your mouth, blow hard to push any water out of it, and breathe in.

Your limbs feel weak and your joints hurt, but you force yourself to swim toward the *Ocho Reales*. You feel as if you're moving in slow motion, and it seems to take forever.

You are so dazed that you almost swim past the extra air-tanks and slate suspended from your boat. At first it's as though they just don't register on your brain. You take the pencil tied to the slate and painfully scrawl: "GOT BENDS. KATE IN TROUBLE." You jerk the line twice and watch the slate slowly rise.

Turn to page 76.

This time *you* bang on your tanks to bring Kate to the cave. She swims over to find you writing "FOLLOW ME" on your slate. You both swim into the opening of the cave. The opening widens, then turns up at an angle. Finally the narrow passage becomes a large open area. Several small holes above you let light in. Straight ahead, though, you are amazed to see a large steel building—an underwater habitat—taking up the entire back half of the coral cave.

Turn to page 89.

You're not sure how long you hang there. Then Beech is shaking you. He holds the slate in front of your face. "WHERE'S KATE?" You look at it stupidly for a moment; then the fog in your brain lifts. You take the slate and draw a quick map.

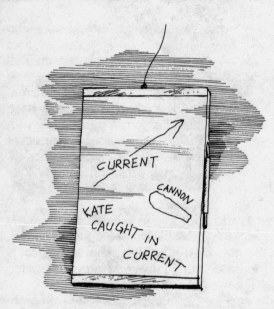

Then you faint.

Turn to page 82.

"We're getting out of here!" you tell Macaulay. "Lightening the bow will help." You both heave the spare anchor overboard. You race to the controls and put the *Ocho Reales* in full reverse. There is a terrible crunching and tearing sound, but with the bow lighter, the boat finally comes off the reef.

You back up the *Ocho Reales* and duck into the other channel. Just in time! The white boat comes close enough to fire shots, but they all miss. For five minutes more you weave and dogde through the maze of coral. As you put more distance between you and the white boat, you realize you're going to run into trouble with the gray boat. They have positioned themselves where you'll leave the reef. If you stop, though, the white boat will catch up to you.

Then Macaulay starts shouting and jumping up and down. "Yahoo! Yahoo!"

"What's going on?" you yell, but then you see for yourself. A Coast Guard helicopter is flying in, and the gray boat is leaving. The white boat is trying to back through the coral maze, but it's too late. It'll never get out of the coral in time.

You stop the *Ocho Reales*'s engines, drop anchor, and slump into the pilot's chair. Your heart is still pounding. Macaulay comes aft. "Now all we have to do," he says, "is find our way out of this maze, pick up Kate and Captain Beech, and go treasure diving."

You smile up at him. "Piece o' cake, Macaulay. Piece o' cake."

The End

"Macaulay, we'll try your plan," you say. "How did this boat keep the two chase boats headed toward each other?"

"I don't know. They just sort of kept zigging and zagging."

"That's not much help, Macaulay." In spite of your situation, you both laugh. Then you say, "I guess we can give it a try." You try zigging to the left. Both boats change course and keep heading right at you. Then you zag to the right. The gray boat changes course first; then the white boat follows. Both boats are much closer now. Even without binoculars you can see men with rifles on the decks.

"I don't think this is going to work," you say to Macaulay as the first shot rings out.

"Duck!" he answers. You duck, but now you can't see too well. The *Ocho Reales* continues straight ahead. You need to change course again for Macaulay's plan to work, but every time you try to get to the wheel, a bullet whizzes near.

"Macaulay, can you fire a flare?"

"Sure, but why?"

"Just do it," you order. At the instant the flare shoots into the sky, you rush to the wheel. You're gambling that everybody will be distracted enough so that you can safely change course.

They are distracted—all but one of them. Just as the *Ocho Reales* responds to the steering wheel, you hear a shot and feel a terrible pain in your midsection. You slump to the deck. It's up to Macaulay now.

The End

"C'mon, Macaulay," you say. "We're going diving."

"Are you crazy?"

"Nope," you answer. "We can't stay here, and they won't follow us underwater."

Just before you splash into the water, you see that the white boat is almost directly behind the *Ocho Reales*. Whew! That was close.

Then you hear a tremendous low noise. You are thrown against some coral, cutting yourself. Your pursuers are throwing dynamite into the water!

There's another explosion, closer this time. Your ears hurt fiercely after this one. Your eardrums must be ruptured. Then there's a third explosion, the closest of all. Your regulator is torn from your mouth. You are twisted through the water and violently scraped against the coral, but you don't feel it at all.

The End

The next thing you know, Beech and Macaulay are by your side. "Kate!" you cry. "She's in a current! Quick!"

Beech puts his hand on your shoulder. "It's all right," he says. "Relax." You look at him, then around you. You're in a hospital bed. "You'll be okay," Beech says. "At least that's what the doctor said. You might have a limp, but it may go away. You were lucky."

"Kate?" you ask in a whisper.

"We never found her," Beech says softly. "She must have been swept away." He shrugs sadly. "There was no trace."

The End

"Macaulay!" you yell. "We've got to leave right away. I have a feeling that boat is Captain Jack's."

Macaulay hurries forward to release the boat from its anchor. You head for the engine controls. The large diesel starts quickly. It may not be as big as the one on Captain Jack's boat, but you know you'll be able to give him a run for his money.

Macaulay rushes over to you. "What about the cannon?" he asks. "We can't get away with that hanging over the side." You know he's right. "I've got the bolt cutters," Macaulay continues. "I can cut the cable and release the cannon."

Your mind races as you try to figure out a way to use the cannon to help your escape. If you drop it right in front of Captain Jack, maybe he'll run over it and damage his boat.

Suddenly you remember Kate and Beech. You must drop some extra scuba tanks over the side for them. There is only enough time to try to sabotage the pirate boat with the cannon or just to cut it free and drop fresh air-tanks to your friends.

The roar of Captain Jack's boat is coming closer. You've got to leave now!

If you try to stop Captain Jack with the cannon, turn to page 109.

If you decide you must get fresh air-tanks to Kate and Beech, turn to page 72.

"Beech, I'm sorry, but we'll use the air lift."

Beech's face falls. "I was afraid you'd say that."

The rest of the day is spent assembling the air lift. The deck becomes a maze of equipment: hundreds of feet of six-inch flexible hose, an equal length of narrow hose to bring air from the compressor, and most important, the sorting tray. Pontoons around its edge keep it afloat, while the fine mesh bottom will collect the sand, debris, and any treasure from the air lift, yet also allow the water to drain away.

The next morning, you and Beech head down to the bottom. Kate stays on the boat to run the compressor. Macaulay is in the water, keeping an eye on the sand and junk that flows from the air lift into the sorting tray, looking for any treasure it might contain.

All that day you labor with the air lift. It's hard work. When you lose track of the air lift's mouth for a second, it buries itself in the sand. You turn it off, clean it out, and start over. It also churns up sand, making it hard to see what is revealed by the suction.

At the end of the day, you have all taken your turn on the air lift, but you've found nothing— nothing at all. Tired and discouraged, you go to bed.

Turn to page 97.

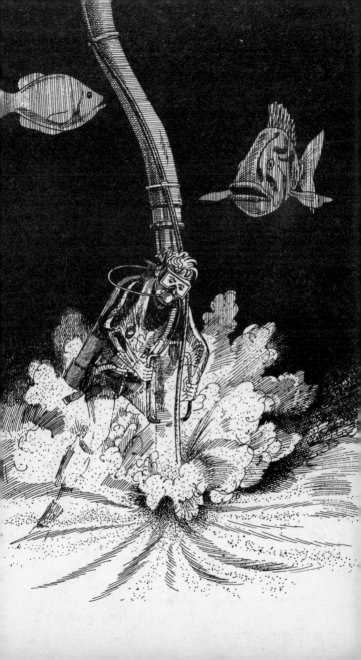

You realize instantly that you have used up your main air supply. You must reach back quickly and pull down the lever on the valve of your regulator to release your reserve supply.

You can't do it! The fishing line is tangled all around your tank—almost like a net. You try again, reaching at a slightly different angle. At first you still can't push down the lever, but by straining to your utmost, you succeed.

Your heart pounds from the effort. You know you have only five minutes more of air. You reach for your knife lying on the bottom below you. Your hand stops inches from it. Again the fishing line won't let you reach what you need. Then you remember the menace of the shark. You think your predicament is hopeless, worse than any nightmare. Still, you strain against the tangled fishing line, reaching out for the knife. Luckily, the shark is not in sight. Perhaps it swam off.

Something nudges you on your shoulder. The shark! You whip your head around, expecting the worst. But it's only Kate, and she's cutting you free.

Turn to page 93.

88

You feel like taking a deep breath and holding it before diving deeper to look for Kate, but you know you shouldn't. This thought makes you want to laugh. You realize you are starting to feel the effects of nitrogen narcosis, the enormous pressure of the water turning the nitrogen gas in your air into a drug.

Then the years of training under Beech's expert guidance exert themselves. By gently blowing against your finger-pinched nose, you equalize the pressure in your ears. Then you blow into your mask, pushing it back out against the water pressure that is squeezing it to your face.

You kick down, deeper into the hole. The water is murky. Your depth gauge glows dimly: 220 feet. There's no sign of Kate. You continue kicking.

"This is fun!" you think. "The tunnel looks like a carnival ride. I'm even dizzy!" You giggle a little. "What am I doing here?" Then you remember. Kate! You've got to find Kate! You look at your depth gauge: 250 feet. There's something wrong about that, but you can't recall what. "Kate's deeper. Kate's deeper," you say to yourself. "I've got to get her." But something is nagging at you to turn around and ascend.

If you keep going deeper, looking for Kate, turn to page 24.

If you try to ascend, turn to page 104.

"What is this building? And who would have built such a thing?" you ask yourself. You check your depth gauge: you're 30 feet below the surface of the bay.

Swimming along the floor of the cave, you move closer to the steel structure. It is a semicircular tube, butting up against the back wall of the cave. The top half of the tube is larger in diameter than the bottom half; it overhangs the lower half by about ten feet. You swim under the overhang. Ten feet above you is a short steel ladder coming out of a round opening in the overhang. An entrance! There is no need of a door. You know that the inside of the structure must be pressurized to the 20-foot level, keeping the water out. A diver can climb in and out of the hole, finding air above and water below. At a depth of 20 feet, someone can live indefinitely without worrying about decompression.

Turn to page 92.

"Beech, I'm coming down," you shout. Hurriedly you put on your tanks while Kate hands Beech a fresh tank of air.

You grab a new tank for Macaulay and a pry bar, and splash into the water. Beech leads the way. You are anxious for Macaulay, knowing he must be scared. Near the bottom, Beech suddenly stops, then grabs you and starts pulling you back. You wonder what's going on. The water ahead is murky, but you make out a moving shape. A shark! And no Macaulay—or not much of him anyway.

Quickly, but carefully, you swim away. You guess at what might have happened. The sharp coral around the cannon must have cut Macaulay's trapped foot. The blood attracted the shark, and Macaulay, alone, his foot caught, didn't stand a chance.

As you return to the surface you realize that while Beech found the cannon, you'd rather have no cannon than no Macaulay. You don't think you have the stomach for any more exploration.

The End

Kate taps you on the arm. On her slate is written: "WHY IS THIS HERE?" You've got a suspicion. This probably isn't a scientific or experimental underwater habitat; it is too well hidden in the middle of the coral for that. You have a feeling that it is a smuggler's hideout. Could this have something to do with the dreaded Captain Jack?

Maybe you'd better leave right away. Who knows if someone is inside, watching you? Still, there's no sign of anyone, and you're intensely curious to see what's inside the habitat.

If you decide to enter the strange habitat, turn to page 34.

If you decide you'd better leave the cave as quickly as possible, turn to page 28.

You feel wobbly as you swim back to the boat with Kate. You use up the last of your reserve air on the way and must buddy-breathe—share Kate's air—to make it. Once you're back on board the *Ocho Reales*, you gobble huge amounts of fresh air as if you can't get enough.

You know you'll go back down eventually—after all, the necklace proves that the treasure exists—but for now all you want to do is sit in the sun and breathe good clean air.

The End

Finally, the full twenty-three minutes have passed. You grab your slate and write another message to Kate: "I LIED. ASCEND NOW." As soon as you're both on the *Ocho Reales'* deck, you shout, "Let's get out of here!"

Beech starts the big diesel while you turn on the radio. You're flying out of the bay at twenty-five knots by the time you get the Coast Guard on the radio. Beech and Macaulay listen incredulously as they hear you describe to the authorities the underwater cave with the steel habitat.

"Roger, *Ocho Reales*, we copy," the guardsman says when you're done. "We'll take care of it. Stay out of trouble." That's what you intend to do, anyway. "And thank you. We've been trying to find Captain Jack's hideout for a long time."

"How do you feel?" Beech asks you and Kate. "Any sign of the bends?" You both shake your heads no.

Go on to the next page.

"What's this chest?" Macaulay asks, having retrieved it from your equipment.

"I forgot about it," you say.

"Me, too," Kate adds.

"Well, open it!" Beech says impatiently. Macauley sticks a pry under the lid and the flimsy lock pops open. Doubloons! You can't believe your eyes. The smugglers must have explored the area around the hideout many times and, bit by bit, discovered some of the coins from the lost Spanish fleet.

You've found your treasure after all.

The End

The next morning, you start out working the air lift. All day you labor as before, and the next day, and the next. Each spot you investigate yields no treasure. You do find a couple of cannonballs, a cannon, and Captain Rounder's anchor, but that's not what you are after. You begin to wonder if there's any treasure at all.

On the last dive of the fourth day, Beech is working the air lift. You are down below with him, keeping an eye on what he uncovers. Suddenly, there's the glint of metal. Beech stops the air lift. You use your hands to dig through the sand. Shaking with excitement, you uncover a disk! You pull it free. It's about eight inches across and three inches thick, and it's solid gold!

You surface with your find to show it to Kate and Macaulay. Kate hurries it to the scales. "It weighs ten pounds!" she shouts. With renewed energy you dive back to the bottom.

Now it seems as if the sea floor is paved with precious metal. Practically everywhere you dig you turn up something. Masses of gold doubloons, more giant gold disks, hunks of sea-corroded silver, tableware, gold and silver jewelry, all come to the surface to join the growing mound of treasure.

Go on to the next page.

You look in amazement at the riches you have found. You will split the treasure five ways: one share to each of the crew, and one to the *Ocho Reales* for repairs, new equipment, and the financing of other adventures.

You estimate your share with a practiced eye. It should come to eight or nine million dollars. You wonder what you'll do with all that money. You could retire from the dangers of treasure hunting for the rest of your life. You could do just about anything you want—including nothing. But you have a growing suspicion that for you *searching* for treasure—any kind of treasure—may be more reward than finding it.

The End

GOLDEN

DOUBLOON

You walk up to the door and spin the locking wheel. The door swings open on silent hinges. You step into a small room. There are brocade chairs, small tables with beautiful crystal lamps, and a red velvet couch. A Persian rug covers the steel floor. Off the room you can see a small kitchen and bedroom.

"Why, it's a little apartment," Kate says from behind you. "It's a hideout," you correct her. "And a dollar says it belongs to Captain Jack."

Go on to the next page.

"Don't take that bet," a voice calls from the bedroom. "You'll lose for sure." A short, fat man steps into the living room.

Turn to page 103.

You flick on your underwater flashlight. The beam shoots out into the water for about fifteen feet. There are white particles floating everywhere, reflecting the light, making it impossible to see. You wave the flashlight around, hoping Kate will see it. The white particles surround you. You take a closer look at one. It's a small shrimp. There are hundreds—thousands—*millions*—of them!

You are lost in wonder at the number. Why are they here? Then you remember the current. It must bring down tons of water laden with nutrients which feed the shrimp.

You notice a slow movement below you. Kate! The shrimp undulate away in waves as something rises up out of the deep water.

The beam of your light stabs out, stopping on a large arrow-shape moving up near you. Not Kate. Your stomach starts to flutter. All of a sudden you remember the law of the sea: what eats, gets eaten. Something feeds on all these shrimp, and here it is.

Turn to page 111.

"How'd you get here?" Kate blurts out.

"The same way you did," the man replies coolly, rubbing his lips with his left hand. His right hand is in the pocket of the midnight-blue silk Chinese robe he's wearing. "You know," he continues, "in adventure stories this is when the villain reveals the whole story. I suppose it can't do any harm, at this point, to let you in on my little secret. I am"—he smiles crookedly—"Captain Jack, and I am something of a gem trader. I do a nice little business. This 'hideout,' as you call it, is a necessity. There are some in my profession who envy my success."

As he talks, you and Kate are edging back toward the bulkhead door. "No, I'm afraid you won't be leaving," he says. Now you see the automatic pistol in his right hand. "Sorry."

There are two small noises from the gun. You and Kate drop to the floor, still dripping water—and now blood—onto the expensive Persian rug.

The End

104

You turn around and head up toward the tiny bright opening of the hole. As you ascend, your head seems to clear. "I've got to get back to the boat and get Beech and Macaulay. Together we'll find Kate," you say to yourself.

Then, above you, a stripe appears through the murky water—two stripes—the markings on Kate's tank and wetsuit. You must have passed her on the way down. Kate hangs there, motionless. You realize that she's unconscious. You can see the bubbles slowly rising from her regulator. At least she's breathing! You've got to get her—and yourself—out of these depths and back to the boat.

Carefully, so as not to knock it out of her mouth, you press your hand against her regulator, ensuring that in her unconscious state she can continue to breathe. Then, slowly and cautiously, you swim the two of you up to the light.

You stay over toward the edge of the hole, out of the main force of the current. The swimming is still difficult, though, and you are glad to pop out of the hole.

Turn to page 108.

106

"What is it?" Kate asks. You put the black rock on the deck and tap it with a hammer. It breaks open. Inside, silver flashes in the sunlight.

"It is—or was—a bunch of silver coins in a wooden chest. See how the lump has square corners? The sea water disintegrated the container and oxidized the silver, turning it black and sticking it together."

"Does this mean we've found the treasure?" Macaulay asks, his coral cuts forgotten for the moment.

Go on to the next page.

"We can't be sure yet," you answer. "We have to clean these coins up and examine the dates and mint marks. We also have to check that cannon closely." You heft the chunk of silver. "We definitely found some treasure, but maybe not *the* treasure. This could be from one of the warships guarding the fleet and not from one of the treasure ships. It could even be from an entirely different wreck. We have a lot of work left."

"Oh, don't be a spoilsport," Kate interrupts. For an answer you just smile back at her, and the next thing you know you're dancing around in a circle singing, "We're in the money, we're in the money!"

The End

Keeping well away from the current, you swim as fast as you can back to the *Ocho Reales*. It's not easy, and after a while you check your pressure gauge. You're running out of air! You check Kate's gauge. She's got a little more than you, but not much. You know you can't surface because you must stay pressurized in order to avoid the bends. In fact, you suddenly realize, you'll have to stay down for about two hours in order to avoid the crippling disease. You sure hope Beech has those extra air-tanks hanging in the water!

You tear your eyes away from the pressure gauge and, holding Kate carefully, move your flippers in slow powerful kicks. Every ounce of air counts now.

You run out of air in your main supply. You reach back and pull down the reserve lever on your tank. You will yourself to remain calm and breathe as shallowly as possible.

Your muscles are burning. The breathing gets harder. Suddenly there's no more air. You must surface and risk the bends, or drown. There's no air left to inflate your buoyancy compensator. You pull the quick release on your weight belt and drop it. At the same moment something grips your flipper. You can't ascend!

Turn to page 50.

"Macaulay," you shout, "wait for my signal before cutting the cannon loose. I'm going to try something." Macaulay runs aft while you watch Captain Jack's boat approach on your starboard side, waiting for the right moment.

Quickly you pull the throttles to maximum. The engine growls and the *Ocho Reales* shudders from stem to stern as it strains to move against the weight of the cannon. Slowly the boat gathers speed forward. The cannon resists, swinging aft. Then, gathering momentum, it starts to swing forward.

You pull the wheel over to the right, running right across Captain Jack's path. "Cut it now!" you shout to Macaulay. The cannon swings heavily inward toward the hoist itself, before Macaulay can cut it free. There is a tearing noise as the bolts holding the hoist down to the deck start to tear out. The hoist starts toppling. The *Ocho Reales* tips sideways. The wheel won't respond! You're foundering in Captain Jack's path!

Turn to page 112.

110

You run forward to see what damage there is. "Can we rock it off?" you ask Macaulay.

"Maybe. It's not too bad."

You look back at the white boat. It's slowly getting closer. Your pursuers aren't moving as fast through the coral as you were, but now they can see that you're aground. You turn back to Macaulay. "If we get loose, is there another route to take?"

His answer is quick. "Yes. There were two ways to go back there." He points, then shrugs. "This one looked better."

There's just enough time to try the other channel and stay away from Captain Jack's henchmen—if you can get off the spot you're grounded on quickly enough. You can't stay here—but then you realize there is an alternative. You could dive.

If you try the other channel through the coral, turn to page 77.

If you decide you'd better get off the boat and into the water, turn to page 80.

The arrow-shape continues moving. It's a squid! But not an ordinary squid; it's a giant squid. It must be eight feet across! Its body keeps rising, rising until it's as tall above you as a house.

Now you can see the tentacles below you, stretching out beyond the length of the light beam. They're moving, shoveling up food and pushing it toward the squid's huge beak. A giant sucker attaches to you and directs you into the gaping mouth.

The End

There is a tremendous crash as the gray boat runs right into the middle of the *Ocho Reales*, cutting it almost in two.

Go on to the next page.

As you are thrown to the deck, you realize the *Ocho Reales* is already starting to sink. You wonder where Macaulay is. You don't spot him before the *Ocho Reales* is blown apart as the gray boat explodes.

The pressure wave from the explosion travels swiftly through the water to alert Kate and Beech. They swim over as fast as they can, but it's too late. There are no survivors.

The End

ABOUT THE AUTHOR

Julius Goodman lives in Vermont and is a writer, editor, and designer of books. He was educated at McGill University and Emerson College. He has also written *Space Patrol* and *The Horror of High Ridge*, other Bantam Choose Your Own Adventure® books.

ABOUT THE ILLUSTRATOR

Paul Granger is a prize-winning illustrator and painter.

DO YOU LOVE CHOOSE YOUR OWN ADVENTURE®?

Let your younger brothers and sisters in on the fun.

You know how great CHOOSE YOUR OWN ADVENTURE® books are to read and reread. But did you know that there are CHOOSE YOUR OWN ADVENTURE® books for younger kids too? They're just as thrilling as the CHOOSE YOUR OWN ADVENTURE® books you read and they're filled with the same kinds of decisions and different ways for the stories to end— but they're shorter with more illustrations and come in a larger, easier-to-read size.

So get your younger brothers and sisters and anyone else you know between the ages of seven and nine in on the fun by introducing them to the exciting world of CHOOSE YOUR OWN ADVENTURE.® They're on sale wherever Bantam paperbacks are sold.

AV10